101 AESOP'S FABLES

For Children

THIS BOOK BELONGS TO

----

5 MINUTES
READ ALOUD
ILLUSTRATED
TALES WITH
MORALS

Wonder House

Wonder House
(An imprint of Prakash Books)

contact@wonderhousebooks.com

ISBN : 978-93-54404-77-1

Contents

1. The Lion and the Mouse

Once upon a time, there lived a lion in a beautiful dense forest. He was widely known for his kindness. One day, the lion was resting after lunch when a tiny mouse started disturbing him.

The lion woke up, quite irritated. He pounced on the rat and grabbed him tightly. 'Please forgive me, my Lord! Let me go and I will return the favor when the time is right,' begged the terrified mouse. The lion was quite amused, thinking how a tiny mouse could help him, ever. But being a generous king, he let him go.

One morning, the lion was taking a walk in the jungle and got trapped in a net laid by a hunter. He struggled to free himself and started roaring so loud that the whole jungle shivered with fear.

The tiny mouse recognized the roar and ran to see him. He got down to work immediately and started chewing the ropes of the net with his sharp teeth.

The lion was relieved to be free and thanked the mouse. The two became best friends from that day onwards.

Moral: We should always be kind to others.

2. Who will Bell the Cat?

In the forest of Catoland, animals lived in joy and harmony. But the mice were not happy at all. A big, fat cat was a menace to them. The cat would hunt down the mice stealthily. The mice lived in constant fear of being attacked.

One day, the mice called for an urgent meeting to find a solution to the problem. They sat around their King and Queen and started discussing plans.

‘The cat is smart. She pounces upon us from anywhere,’ a mouse spoke. ‘Yes, we don’t hear her footsteps,’ said another. They all agreed and offered several solutions, but nothing gained acceptance.

Then a young mouse stood up and said, 'Why don't we bell the cat? Then when we hear the bell, we will know that she is around.'

Everyone was surprised by the sheer genius of the idea. Of course, once the cat was belled, the mice could run to safety. The Queen, who was listening intently to everything, spoke, 'Oh! I really appreciate the idea. But tell me who will bell the cat?'

The mice were all crestfallen and sulked.

Moral: It is one thing to propose something, but quite different executing it.

3. The Frogs and the Ox

Once upon a time, there was a family of frogs that lived in a clear pond. One day, an ox came to drink water and accidentally crushed one of the baby frogs.

The mother frog soon missed her little one and started looking for it. She asked the other babies about the missing child. The children informed her that a huge monster had stepped on their sibling and had killed it.

The mother frog was devastated and asked how big that monster was. The kids replied that it was very big. The mother frog puffed up her body and asked, ‘Was the monster this big?’

‘No, mom!’ replied the babies. ‘It was bigger.’

The sad and angry mother swelled her body more, so that she could get an idea of the monster’s size. In her grief, she kept on puffing her body more and more and the kids kept repeating that the monster was still bigger. Alas! Her sad mind and bloated body could take no more and she burst, trying to know the size of the monster.

Moral: We should be wise and know our limits.

4. The Fox and the Grapes

Foxy, the clever fox, was going to his Granny's house for summer vacations. His mother sent gifts for Granny but forgot to pack grapes. Granny and Foxy both loved grapes a lot. So Foxy planned to get some on his way to her house.

It was noon, and the heat made Foxy very tired. He wanted to rest somewhere. Suddenly, something caught his attention. It was a grapevine laden with juicy grapes.

'Ah! Such delicious grapes! Granny will be happy to eat them,' thought Foxy. Licking his lips, he jumped as high as he could but without luck. He even ran and leaped towards the grapes but to no avail. Not ready to give up, he tried repeatedly but failed.

By this time, poor Foxy was hungry. He attempted everything but couldn't be successful.

'Why am I trying for these grapes? They are sour anyway!' Foxy consoled himself and started his journey once more.

Moral: We should always keep on trying, even if we fail at times.

5. The Wolf and the Crane

Once there was a glutton wolf who gobbled up his food very fast. He would swallow down everything, even the bones.

One day, the wolf was invited to a party in the forest. As usual, he started gobbling up the food quickly. Suddenly, a bone got stuck in his throat. He made all efforts to swallow it down or spit it out but he couldn't. The animals at the party were horrified.

Then the wolf spotted a crane with a long neck and beak. He requested the crane to pull the bone out of his mouth. He also promised to reward him for the help.

The crane was quite scared to put his beak inside the wolf's mouth. But he was lured by the prospect of a reward. He summoned all his courage and pulled the bone out of the wolf's neck.

The wolf was relieved and started to walk away. The crane called out to him and reminded him of the reward. 'What reward? Aren't you happy that I didn't bite off your neck? That was the reward,' the wolf replied.

Moral: Stay true to your word and be grateful to the ones who helped you.

6. The Heron

Once there was a majestic heron, and he was very difficult to please. He had his own opinion on everything and did things as he liked.

One fine morning, he went to the stream to catch his breakfast. The stream was overflowing with swarms of fish of every kind. But the heron was not in the mood for small fries. He was looking for something big and fleshy.

A perch swam past him but the heron didn't think it was good enough to eat. 'I will wait for something better,' he thought proudly.

Soon, the stream had no fish at all. The heron was quite hungry and irritated now. He saw a small and smelly snail coming towards him slowly. He could not hold himself back anymore and gladly ate the snail as his breakfast. He had learned his lesson.

Moral: We should grab the opportunity at the right time.

7. The Gnat and the Bull

Once there lived a tiny gnat in a meadow. He was under the impression that his voice was the loudest in the whole world. He used to strut around buzzing here and there.

One day, the gnat was flying over the meadow and saw a huge bull resting near a clear stream. 'Let's have some fun and disturb the bull's sleep,' he thought, smiling mischievously.

He sat on the bull's horn and started buzzing at the top of his voice. But the bull did not move. After a long while, his vocal cords were about to burst. Surprisingly, the bull remained undisturbed.

The gnat decided to fly away. Before flying, he said to the bull, 'You must be really glad to have me leave now. My voice must have disturbed your sleep.' He strutted around as he said so.

'Ah! Who are you? Were you here for a long time? I didn't notice anything,' said the sleepy bull.

The gnat was crestfallen.

Moral: The smaller the mind, the greater the egotism.

8. The Plane Tree

Two travelers were walking through a vast plain, looking for a place to rest. They were tired and sweating under the hot sun. Soon they found a big tree that had a large canopy-like shade. They stopped underneath it and sat down to enjoy their food. Once they were full, they lay down and noticed that they were lying under a Plane Tree.

'How worthless this plane tree is! It bears no flower or fruit. It only serves to litter the ground by shedding leaves,' said one.

'What a waste!' agreed the other.

'Good Lord! How ungrateful you creatures are!' came an angry voice from the plane tree. 'You people had food and are resting under my shade, yet you find me worthless. Perhaps, you don't count your blessings.'

The two friends were shocked to death and ran away leaving their stuff behind.

Moral: We should be grateful for our blessings.

9. The Owl and the Grasshopper

The nocturnal owl was getting old now. She would sleep most of the time and get angry if someone disturbed her slumber. Even during the night, she hardly went out to hunt for food. So she ate whatever came her way.

One hot afternoon, the old owl was dozing off in her house. Suddenly, a young grasshopper started singing loudly. The old owl woke up irritated. She shouted from her window, 'Can you stop singing now? Can't you see I am resting?'

'You don't own the place. I have as much right to this place as you,' said the proud grasshopper.

The owl realized that she cannot overpower him as it was daytime. She softened her voice and said, 'You are right. Now that I am awake, I should rather enjoy your beautiful song. Why don't you come inside and have something to sweeten your throat?'

The grasshopper got flattered and jumped into the owl's hole. Now the owl could see him clearly in the darkness. She pounced on him and ate him up immediately.

Moral: Don't get tricked by flattery.

10. The Oak and the Reeds

A giant oak tree and some reeds were good friends. They grew near a stream. The oak tree was proud of his size and strength. The reeds were soft, small and humble.

The oak tree always stood against the blowing winds and refused to bow down. He would make fun of the reeds, who bent down in the wind. 'We bow down to save ourselves from breaking,' the humble reeds would reply. They would warn the oak tree against standing upright in a storm but he paid no heed.

One evening, a strong thunderstorm blew. The giant oak tree prepared itself for the onslaught. 'Please bend down a little. The winds will break you,' cried the reeds, who were already bent down. 'Not at all! The thunderstorm can do me no harm,' hollered the oak.

The thunderstorm heard him and grew fierce. He blew with all his strength and uprooted the proud oak tree. The oak tree fell on the ground with a loud thud and died.

Moral: We should be grateful for our blessings.

11. The Owl and the Grasshopper

One hot afternoon, a thirsty crow was flying in the sky, searching for water. The sun had become harsh and unbearable. He flew over barren lands with no trace of water in sight.

As he neared a village, he spotted a pitcher under a tree. Relieved, the crow flew down and perched on the rim of the pitcher. He could see some water at the bottom.

The crow tried to put his beak inside but couldn't reach the water level. It was too low. He got restless and tried putting his head inside yet he couldn't take a sip. No matter how hard he tried, he failed every time.

Suddenly, he saw some pebbles lying close by. An idea crossed his mind. He picked up the pebbles and began to drop them one-by-one into the pitcher. Slowly, the water level started rising. At last, the water reached a level where the crow could drink it easily. He quenched his thirst and flew away feeling satisfied.

Moral: Your cleverness can save you from trying times.

12. The Fox and the Stork

There was a forest who was witness to a strange friendship between a fox and a stork. One day, the fox decided to play a prank on his friend. He invited the stork for dinner at his den.

The stork was on time for dinner. The fox served a delicious soup in a shallow plate. 'It smells yummy!' said the stork and dipped his beak into the plate. But no matter how hard he tried, he could not take a sip with his long bill.

The cunning fox enjoyed the soup delightfully. The stork was angry but kept calm. Before leaving, he invited the fox for lunch at his place.

The fox paid the stork a visit the next day. The stork served an aromatic dish made from fish in a tall, narrow jar. The annoyed fox sniffed and licked the rim of the jar but couldn't eat. On the other hand, the stork used his long bill and enjoyed the fish.

Once done, the stork said, 'When you make fun of others, be prepared for the same.'

Moral: Do not humiliate others as you can face the same.

13. The Stag and His Reflection

Once upon a time, there lived a stag who was very proud of his looks, especially his long and beautiful antlers. The only thing that the stag did not like was his skinny, spindly legs and was quite ashamed of them.

'How can I have such lanky legs and a beautiful crown on my head?' the stag would wonder.

One afternoon, the stag was drinking water from a pond and was admiring the reflection of his antlers. Suddenly, he felt the presence of a panther behind him. In a moment, the stag took to his legs and shot off into the forest.

The panther ran after him, chasing him deep inside the forest. The stag ran ahead but, alas, his antlers got stuck in the branches of a tree. Soon, the panther caught up with him and pounced upon him.

The poor stag realized that his ugly legs could have saved him but his ornamental antlers cut short his life.

Moral: What we don't appreciate is sometimes worth a lot.

14. The Rooster and the Fox

One evening, an old, wise rooster flew to his favorite tree to take rest. He crowed twice and was about to put his head under his wings when he saw a fox come by. 'Hello, dear friend!' the fox greeted the rooster. 'Have you heard about the peace treaty in the jungle?'

'What peace treaty?' asked the rooster, wary of the sly fox.

The fox elaborated, 'From now on, there will be no enmity between us. We can trust each other and live in peace.'

He invited the rooster to come down and celebrate with a tight hug. The rooster said, 'That's great! Let's wait for some more friends to join in. I can see the hounds coming this way. Perhaps they have heard the good news too.'

The fox immediately took to his heels saying, 'I forgot about a very important errand. Besides, the hounds live deep inside the jungle. They might not have heard about the treaty yet.'

The rooster smiled to himself and went off to sleep.

Moral: Do not trust sweet talkers and be smart before taking any action.

15. The Fox and the Goat

The summers were getting very hot and dry in the forest. A thirsty fox was looking for water and found a shallow well. He was so desperate to drink water that he lost his balance and fell into the well. He tried everything but couldn't get out of it.

A goat soon reached there, looking for water. She peeped inside and saw the fox. Foolish as she was, she thought that the fox was enjoying himself. She asked him, 'Is the water cool?'

'Oh yes! The water is indeed very cool and sweet. You must come here. We can enjoy it together,' said the cunning fox.

The goat was taken in by the luring words of the fox and jumped inside. The fox was waiting for this opportunity only. He climbed on the goat's back and leaped out of the well.

The poor goat cried for help but the fox replied, 'You should have found a way to get out of the well, before jumping inside. Why did you trust me blindly?'

Moral: Look before you leap.

16. The Two Goats

A herd of goats once lived in a mountain valley. A deep river flowed through the valley, separating the steep mountain slopes. The only means of crossing the river was an old tree trunk that had fallen over the river, making a bridge. But it was so narrow that not even the smallest of animals dared to step on it.

One day, two goats were crossing the river at the same time, one from each end of the trunk. One of them said, 'Move back! I stepped on the bridge first.'

'You should step back. I am older than you,' argued the other. 'But I am stronger than you,' replied the first one.

Both the goats refused to budge. They stepped closer towards each other and locked horns in the middle of the bridge. They fought and pushed each other. But it was not long before the two stubborn goats lost balance and fell into the river. Both of them were swept away by the river.

Moral: It is better to yield than to bear loss because of stubbornness.

17. The Frog and the Mouse

A young mouse lived near a pond with his family. He would often roam along the edge of the pond, wishing to explore more. A mischievous frog lived across the pond.

One day, the frog asked the mouse, 'Hello friend! Would you like to visit my house?'

'I would love to,' replied the excited mouse. 'But I cannot swim. Will you help me?' The frog immediately agreed and tied one leg of the mouse to his own with a reed. Then he jumped into the pond, dragging the mouse along.

Soon, the mouse got tired and gave up. He wanted to return to land. But the frog had other plans. He pulled the mouse in the middle of the pond and drowned him.

The frog then began to untie the reed that bound him to the dead mouse. A hungry hawk was hovering over the pond. She noticed a dead mouse floating on the surface and swooped down to pick it up. Soon, the dead mouse along with the dangling frog became a delicious meal for the hawk.

Moral: Those who wish harm for others, sometimes get trapped in their own ploy.

18. The Wolf in Sheep's Clothing

Once, a shepherd had a flock of sheep in his farm. Every day, he would take them out to graze in the pasture and bring them back safely into the fold. A wolf, who lived close to the pasture, was always looking for ways to attack the sheep. But the alert shepherd foiled all his attempts.

The wolf feared that he could die of starvation if he didn't find a solution soon. One day, he got lucky as he found a sheepskin that had been cast away. The wolf immediately wore the sheepskin and slipped into the flock of sheep without being noticed. He planned to stay in the fold and kill one sheep every night.

That evening, the shepherd decided to throw a party at home. His wife wanted to cook mutton curry and asked him to get a sheep. As destiny willed, the first sheep that the shepherd laid his hands on, was the wolf in sheepskin. Alas! The wolf was killed and chopped into pieces.

Moral: Deceit never pays.

19. The Hare and the Tortoise

A hare and a tortoise lived in the forest with other animals. They were good friends but the hare often made fun of the tortoise for being slow.

One day, the tortoise challenged the hare to a race. 'I may be slow but I can defeat you in a race,' he said. The hare was amused but he agreed for the sake of fun. The venue was decided and all the animals gathered to cheer the two friends. Mr. Fox marked the distance and flagged off the race.

The hare ran with all his might and was soon out of sight. As he neared the finish line, he decided to rest and wait for the tortoise, to ridicule him. Before long, he dozed off and started snoring.

In the meanwhile, the tortoise kept walking slowly but steadily. Soon, he passed the hare and was very close to the finish line.

After a peaceful nap, the hare woke up and started running rapidly, when he saw the tortoise reaching the end of the race. But it was too late for him. The tortoise crossed the finish line first and won the race.

Moral: Slow and steady wins the race.

20. The Fox and the Crow

One fine day, a sly fox was out in the jungle looking for breakfast. He saw a crow sitting on a tree with a delicious piece of cheese in her break. The fox was filled with greed and decided to snatch it from her. 'Hello dear!' he greeted the crow. 'A beautiful day, isn't it?'

The crow was aware of the fox's cunningness. So she didn't pay any attention to what he said.

The fox was disappointed but he didn't give up. He said again, 'What beautiful feathers you have! They look so bright and glossy.'

This time the crow listened with attention but didn't open her mouth. The fox made a final attempt and said, 'You are the most gracious bird around. If only you could sing as beautifully as you look, I would hail you as the queen of all birds.'

Flattered by the compliments, the crow lost all her intelligence and gave the loudest caw to please the fox. The piece of cheese dropped down straight into the fox's open mouth. He enjoyed it thoroughly while the crow was left wondering at his wits.

Moral: Flatterers are not trustworthy.

21. The Dog and His Reflection

One day, a dog was sitting outside a butcher's shop waiting for a piece of bone. The butcher had been watching him since morning and threw the biggest bone at him. The dog grabbed the bone and ran towards his house.

He had to cross a narrow footbridge to reach home. He was careful not to drop the bone in the lake. But as he reached halfway through the bridge, he happened to look down into the water and saw his own reflection. His greed got the better of him and he thought it was another dog with a bigger piece of bone than his. He couldn't wait to have that piece as well.

The dog opened his mouth to bark at the dog in water and the bone dropped into the lake. He immediately leaped into the water, to snatch the bigger bone, but found nothing. The lake was deep and the dog somehow managed to swim to safety.

Alas! He lost his prize because of his greed.

Moral: Greediness can be very costly.

22. The Mother and the Wolf

A shepherd once lived in a village with his wife and a newly-born baby. He had two fierce dogs who guarded his sheep.

One morning, a wolf came prowling in search of prey near the cottage. He overheard the mother telling her baby, 'Hush, Hush girl! If you don't stop crying, I will give you to the wolf.'

The wolf was overjoyed to hear this. He thought, 'I did the right thing by coming here. I will get to eat a soft and delicious meal today.'

He kept on waiting all afternoon under an open window. As time passed, he started growing uneasy with hunger.

When evening approached, the mother settled near the window to rock her baby to sleep. She lovingly told her baby, 'My little darling, I will never give you to the wolf. Papa will kill the wolf, if he ever tries to come near us.'

The wolf felt cheated but had to escape as the father returned home with two dogs.

Moral: Don't believe all that you hear.

23. The Ant and the Dove

One day, an ant went to a brook to drink water. Unfortunately, she slipped and fell into the water. She tried to swim to the bank but in vain. She was on the verge of drowning when a dove noticed her. She immediately plucked a leaf and dropped it into the water, close to the ant.

The ant climbed onto the leaf which gradually drifted towards the bank. She quickly got off on dry ground and thanked the dove for helping her.

Later, the same day, a hunter came into the jungle looking for birds. The ant noticed him aiming his gun towards the dove who was not watching. Just as he was ready to shoot, the ant bit him on the toe and the hunter missed his aim. The dove got alert and flew away to safety.

Moral: Kindness always pays.

24. The Oxen and the Wheels

A farmer was going to the market to sell wheat. He loaded tons of wheat on his cart. A pair of oxen had to pull all that weight along a muddy road. Though the oxen were bearing the entire load, still they were not complaining. Quietly and patiently, they kept on pulling the cart.

But the wheels of the cart were grumpy. They groaned and sighed and complained about the heavy load. At every turn or bump, they made a sad noise. The oxen were getting annoyed with all that creaks and cranks.

Finally, they could take no more and spoke up, 'Wheels, why are you so grumpy? You don't have to bear that much of weight as we are the ones pulling the cart. Yet, we are doing our job without any complaints. Don't you think that you should just shut up and roll?'

The wheels felt ashamed. They realized their mistake. They kept quiet afterwards and all of them reached the market on time.

Moral: Those who complain the least maybe are suffering the most.

25. The Wolf and the Kid

This is a story about a baby goat who had started growing horns. It made him think that he was a grown-up goat who could be on his own.

One day, he was grazing in the pasture with his mom and the flock. When evening came, the flock started going back home. His mother called out to him but the kid paid no heed and continued nibbling the soft grass. Soon the flock left and the kid was all alone.

It was dark all around. Suddenly huge shadows and the chilly wind appeared. He knew what was happening. He had heard about the wolf. He started running, calling out his mom. But unfortunately, only the wolf answered his calls.

The kid felt hopeless seeing the wolf standing before him. Yet he gathered courage and said, 'Sir, you will eat me shortly but before that, please play a song on your flute. I want to sing and dance and enjoy before dying.' The wolf agreed and started playing the flute.

The flock had not gone far and they heard the wolf's tune. The shepherd's dogs immediately recognized the wolf's party song and raced back to the pasture to rescue the kid. The wolf at once took to his heels to save his life. He realized that he had been a fool to turn into a musician for a kid, when he should have just eaten him at the first chance.

Moral: Focus on your goals first.

26. The Fisherman and the Little Fish

Once, a fisherman lived in a village with his family. He survived on the fish that he caught and sold in the market.

One day, the fisherman ran out of luck as he couldn't catch a single fish. Hours went by and nothing came in the fishing net. He decided to wrap up his day and was about to leave when he saw a small fry in his net. He picked it up and kept it in the basket.

The little fish spoke up, 'Hey! Why don't you put me back in the water? I am so small. How can I be of any value to you? Let me grow big and then you can catch me again and make good money.'

The fisherman replied, 'Little fish, how can I be so foolish to throw you back in the water? You may be small but you are my only catch today. Something is always better than nothing.' So saying, the fisherman carried the little fish home.

Moral: Sometimes, something is better than nothing.

27. The Tortoise and the Ducks

A lazy tortoise was lying on the grass and watching the other animals running, hopping and flying. He was filled with despair. He wanted to explore the world but he had a heavy shell on his back and short legs which did not allow him to move freely.

Two ducks were passing by and noticed the gloomy tortoise. The tortoise opened his heart before them and the ducks got an idea.

'We can help you see the world,' said the ducks. They gave the tortoise a stick and asked him to hold it in the center with his teeth. The two ducks took hold of it with their beaks, one at each end. They warned the tortoise, 'Don't open your mouth otherwise you will regret it.' So saying, they sailed towards the sky.

A crow was amused with the sight and exclaimed, 'Oh, this must be the King of Tortoises!' 'Of course I am...' the foolish tortoise opened his mouth to speak. But before he could finish, he fell down to the ground and crashed on a rock.

Moral: Foolish arrogance often leads to disaster.

28. The Young Crab and His Mother

One fine day, a mother crab and a baby crab were resting on the beach. They were taking a day off from work. The young crab was playing, walking and tumbling in the sand. The mother crab looked at him and said, 'Why are you walking sideways, dear? That is not the right way to walk. You should always walk with your toes turned out. That way, you can walk straight.'

'I am sorry mom,' said the young crab. 'Please show me how to walk properly. I will learn fast.'

The mother crab started to walk but couldn't walk straight at all. No matter how hard she tried, she could walk sideways only. Not ready to give up, she turned her toes out but tripped and fell. The young crab ran to help her mom, who had hurt her nose badly.

Moral: Don't preach what you cannot practice.

29. The Eagle and the Jackdaw

Once upon a time, there was a jackdaw who was fascinated by an eagle's strength. One day, he saw the eagle swoop down upon a lamb and pull it away with his strong talons to his nest. The jackdaw got under the illusion that he was equally strong and could achieve the feat.

He chose a ram who was enjoying the green pasture at a farm. Imitating the eagle, he swoop down on the ram and tried to pull him with his weak claws. Unfortunately, his claws got tangled in the wool on the ram's back.

While the jackdaw kept trying hard to rise again, the ram hardly noticed his presence and kept on munching the grass.

But the shepherd noticed the fluttering jackdaw and caught hold of him. He clipped his wings and presented him to his kids to play with. The kids were amused and asked their father, 'What is the name of this bird, papa?'

'He is a jackdaw, kids,' replied the shepherd. 'But sometimes, he thinks himself to be an eagle.'

Moral: One should never imitate others blindly.

30. The Dog, the Rooster and the Fox

Once, a dog and a rooster were best friends. They lived on a farm with other animals. One day, they decided to see the world together and left the farm while the other animals were sleeping. They took a road that went through a forest.

When evening came, they decided to look for a safe place to retire for the night. They were lucky to spot a tree that had a hollow trunk. The dog crept inside the trunk while the rooster flew to one of the higher branches of the tree to roost.

The next morning, as the first rays of the sun reached the deep woods, the rooster woke up. He forgot that he was far away from his farm. As was his duty, he stood on his toes, flapped his wings and crowed loudly.

A cunning fox heard the rooster and his eyes twinkled with the thought of a delicious breakfast after a long time. He hurried to the tree where the rooster was resting and said sweetly, 'Hello friend! You are new to this place. Come down and let me give you a welcome hug. We can be great friends.'

The rooster replied, 'Thank you, Mr. Fox! Why don't you come up here and do that? Please go around this tree and my partner will let you in through the door.'

The fox couldn't wait to eat the rooster and went around the tree only to be grabbed by the forever-alert dog.

Moral: Deceivers will always be losers.

31. The Boy and the Hazelnuts

Ron was a little boy who loved hazelnuts. One day, his mother gave him a jar filled with delicious nuts. Ron got so greedy that he put his hand inside the jar and grabbed a fistful of nuts. But when he tried to pull his hand out, it got stuck.

Ron was not ready to give up a single hazelnut out of his fist. At the same time, he was unable to get his hand out. He got irked and made all efforts but nothing worked.

His mother was watching all this patiently. She finally spoke, 'My boy, why don't you leave some hazelnuts in the jar and take only half? That way you can easily take your hand out of the jar and have some nuts too. You can have some more later on.'

Ron realized his mistake and left half of the hazelnuts inside the jar. Later, both he and his mother enjoyed the tasty nuts together.

Moral: Half a portion is better than none.

32. Hercules and the Wagoner

A farmer was going to the market with a wagon full of goods. It had rained the previous night and the oxen were struggling to pull the wagon along the miry road. Suddenly, one of the wheels sank into the muddy rut. The oxen pulled with all their might but the wagon would not move.

The farmer climbed down and inspected the wheel. He got disappointed as he was losing time. He cursed his bad luck and whined continuously but made no effort to get the wheel out of the rut. Then he called the mighty Hercules for help.

Hercules appeared before the farmer and said, 'You have called me for help but have you tried helping yourself? Push the wheel with your shoulder and urge on your oxen.'

The farmer followed the advice and to his great surprise, the wagon glided out of the rut. The farmer had learned his lesson. He expressed his gratitude and rode along happily.

Moral: God helps those who help themselves.

33. The Bundle of Sticks

This is a story of three brothers who were always quarrelling among themselves. Their father tried a lot to unite them but all his efforts went in vain. His heart would break seeing the rift in the house.

One day, the quarrel got worse. The father thought a lot and got an idea. He asked one of the boys to collect eight sticks and bring them to him. He tied the sticks together with a rope. Then he asked all the boys to come one by one and break the bundle of sticks.

Each of them tried their best and applied all the strength but could not succeed. The father then untied the bundle and gave one stick to each one of them and asked to break it. They broke their sticks easily.

The father was smiling while the boys stood confused. 'My dear children,' he said, 'when the sticks were tied together in a bundle, none of you could break it. But when they were divided, you could break them easily. Power lies in unity, not in division. If you stay united and help each other, no one will be able to harm you. But if you are divided, your strength will be equal to a single stick in the bundle, which can be broken easily.'

That day, the sons learned a life lesson and promised to stay united forever.

Moral: Power lies in unity.

34. The Kid and the Wolf

One day, a farmer kept a baby goat on the roof of a shed, to save him from any harm while he was away in the fields. The young kid was quite naughty and made fun of other animals on the farm. The farmer told the kid to keep to himself and not talk to anyone.

After the farmer was gone, the kid jumped around and enjoyed himself on the thatched roof. Suddenly, he saw a wolf lurking on the farm. He started taunting the wolf and made fun of him. He made faces at the wolf and even mocked him. 'Hey kid,' said the wolf calmly, 'it does not bother me one bit. It's not you who is talking to me, but the roof where you are right now. You would not have spoken to me like that if you had been down here with me.'

The kid was speechless with shame for he realized his mistake.

Moral: Know your time and place before saying anything.

35. The Ass and His Driver

One day, a farmer loaded his ass with goods and started walking towards the market to sell them. His path led down a mountainside.

The ass was quite tired walking down the rough terrain with the heavy load. As soon as he caught sight of the market at the foot of the hill, he decided to take his own path.

He turned towards the nearest cliff and was about to leap, when the farmer sensed his intention. He grabbed his tail and tried to pull him back. He tugged at his tail and urged him to stop but the ass was not ready to understand. Stubborn as he was, the ass pulled away with all his strength to break free.

The farmer got tired and said, 'Foolish ass, I am trying to save you from misfortune but you are not ready to understand. Alright then, you can have your way.' The farmer let go of his tail and the ass plunged to his death, rolling down the mountainside.

Moral: Don't let your stubbornness be the cause of your misfortune.

36. The Ass and the Load of Salt

A salt merchant loaded his ass with heavy sacks of salt and drove him back home from the seashore. On the way, they had to cross a shallow stream. Though they had crossed it several times before, but this time the ass slipped and fell into the water.

He scrambled in the water, panting for breath. The merchant quickly helped him get back to his feet but not before much of the salt had melted away.

'Ah! This feels lighter,' thought the ass, realizing that his burden had reduced. He was delighted with the lighter load and trotted back home happily.

Next day, while crossing the stream, the ass remembered what had happened the day before. This time, he purposely fell into the water to lighten his burden. The ass repeated it for days before the merchant realized his intentions. Annoyed, he decided to teach the ass a lesson.

One day, he loaded the ass with sacks full of cotton and drove him through the stream. As always, the ass fell and rolled over in the water to lighten his load. But when he clambered back to his feet, his load had become ten times heavier.

'Ouch! Ouch!' he cried as he was almost crushed under the heavy weight of the cotton that had absorbed a lot of water. He somehow managed to reach home and decided never to repeat the mistake again.

Moral: Cleverness does not always pay.

37. The Town Mouse and the Country Mouse

Once, a town mouse paid a visit to his cousin who lived in the country. At dinner, the country mouse served him wheat stock, roots and acorns. This was all he had to offer but he offered them freely. The town mouse nibbled at the food and said, 'How do you survive on this plain food, brother? You must come with me to town and enjoy the city life.'

The country mouse listened in awe as the town mouse described the luxuries and food in the city. Next morning, the two of them went to the city. There, the town mouse took the country mouse to the dining hall in a mansion. They found the leftovers of a grand feast—jellies, pastries, cheese and cake. The country mouse had never seen such delicious food.

But just as the country mouse was about to taste the delicacies, a cat mewed and the two mice scampered their way to the hiding place. When they felt safe, they ventured back again. But before they could reach the table, the servants had already cleared it and the two had to go to bed with empty stomachs.

The next morning, before leaving, the country mouse said, 'Cousin, my plain food and simple country life is better than these luxuries and the constant fear of being captured. I prefer the peace and security that I get in the country.'

Moral: Peace is more valuable than luxury.

38. The Farmer and the Stork

There was once a stork who was known for his simplicity and trustworthiness. One day, he was approached by a group of crafty cranes. They wanted the stork to accompany them to a nearby field that had been newly planted.

The stork agreed and the birds went to the field to feed. Little did they know that the farmer had laid a net over the field. The birds got entangled in the meshes and the farmer caught them red-handed.

The stork pleaded to the farmer, 'Please, let me go. I am a stork and we are an honorable bird community. These cranes misled me. I did not know they were going to steal.'

The farmer replied, 'You may be true and honest. But you participated in the plan and I caught you stealing with the cranes. So you will have to face the same punishment as them.'

Moral: You are known by the company you keep.

39. The Shepherd Boy and the Wolf

A shepherd boy was hired to look after a flock of sheep. He had to guard the flock while they grazed on the mountain pasture. The master had told him to call the villagers for help if he sensed any danger.

One day, he decided to play a prank to amuse himself. He went to the edge of a cliff and shouted, 'Wolf! Wolf! Please come for help.' The villagers hurried towards the pasture to save the sheep. But when they got there, they realized that they had been duped. The boy laughed his heart out. The villagers felt humiliated but they forgave him.

This happened several times. One evening, while he was returning to the farm, a big wolf appeared out of nowhere and attacked the sheep. The boy shouted for help but this time no one arrived. The villagers thought that it was his prank call again. The wolf killed many sheep and the boy somehow managed to save his own life. He felt miserable but it was too late.

Moral: Your repetitive lies will lose other's trust in you.

40. The Travelers and the Purse

Once upon a time, two travelers were traveling to a remote area together when one of them stumbled upon a purse. He picked it up and looked inside. It was full of gold coins. He was very happy and said, 'Look, I have found this purse full of gold. How lucky am I!'

'Not I, say how lucky are we!' said the other traveler. 'We are traveling together, so we have to share everything, whether good or bad.'

The first traveler got irritated and said, 'I found this purse, so it's mine!'

Suddenly, they heard a mob coming their way, shouting, 'Thief, thief, catch him!'

The traveler with the purse was scared to death. He said, 'We have to hide this purse or we will be beaten to death.'

The other traveler replied, 'We? No, my friend! Say I will be beaten to death because you have the purse. When you are not ready to share the fortunes of the road then why should I share the misfortunes?'

Moral: If we do not share our good fortune, then we must not expect anyone to share our misfortunes.

41. The Lion and the Ass

The lion was the undisputed king of the jungle. He was majestic calm and moved with grace. All the animals in the forest were in awe of him. He always roamed around in the jungle to inquire after the well-being of his people.

That day, he was on his usual round of the jungle. Wherever he went, he was greeted with love and respect. An ass was grazing nearby and he brayed a scornful remark at the passing lion. The ass felt satisfied after passing his comment as he didn't have the wits to appreciate the king's greatness.

The lion overheard the degrading remark. He quietly turned his face to see who spoke it. When he saw that it was the foolish ass, he said, 'Ah, stupid ass! Please keep on grazing.'

The king quietly walked on. He knew that the ass didn't deserve his attention at all.

Moral: Don't mind the remarks of a fool.

42. The Wolf and His Shadow

One fine evening, the wolf was out in the jungle to hunt. The setting sun cast long shadows of everything on the ground. The wolf too appeared hundred times bigger than his actual size.

The wolf was pleased and said, 'Wow, how big and strong I look! I am far stronger and bigger than the lion. Why should I run away from him? He should know the jungle belongs to me.'

So saying, he strutted towards the lion's den. Suddenly, his shadow was completely blotted by something bigger. Within seconds, he was pounced upon by the strong and majestic lion himself.

The lion had sensed the wolf's intentions and attacked him. The poor wolf was struck down by one powerful stroke of the lion's paw. His foolishness brought him to instant death.

Moral: Don't let fanciful thoughts overpower your sense of reality.

43. Two Travelers and a Bear

Two men were traveling together through a forest. Suddenly, a huge bear sprang from behind the bushes and stood before them.

One of the men immediately climbed up a tree to save himself. He did not worry about his friend. The other man lied down on the ground as if dead. He had heard from someone that bears don't touch dead bodies. He controlled his breathing and remained motionless.

The bear sniffed around the man and went away, thinking him to be dead. The man was successful in fooling the bear.

The first man climbed down the tree and asked his fellow traveller, 'I saw the bear whispering something in your ear. What did he say?'

The second man answered, 'He told me that a friend who leaves you in times of adversity is not trustworthy.'

Moral: Misfortune is the test of true friendship.

44. The Boys and the Frogs

One afternoon, two boys were playing near a pond. They were throwing stones in the water. They were competing with each other to find out who could throw the stones the farthest.

The boys were having a good time. But the frogs in the pond were in great trouble. They hid themselves either deep down in the water or ran to the shore. All of them were scared for their lives.

After bearing with the hullabaloo for a long time, the bravest and oldest among the frogs raised his head out of the pond. He said to the boys, 'O children! I know you are playing and enjoying but please think about us too. We are in great pain and afraid for our lives. What is fun for you might be death for us. Please have mercy and stop this game immediately.'

Moral: Never hurt anyone for your enjoyment.

45. The Ants and the Grasshopper

Autumn had arrived and the days were getting cooler and windy. A family of ants was busy drying the grains that they had gathered during summer. They would store the grains for winter.

A hungry grasshopper with a fiddle under his arm begged for some food. The ants were amazed. 'Why are you begging for food?' one of them asked. 'Didn't you collect anything during summer? What were you doing all that time?'

The grasshopper hesitated but finally accepted his mistake. 'I was busy playing music and didn't bother to collect food,' he replied. 'Please help me and give me something to eat.'

The ants declined to help him. 'You didn't think of saving anything for bad days. This is very careless of you. We don't have anything for irresponsible ones like you.'

The ants went back to their work. The disappointed grasshopper left to look for food at some other place.

Moral: Save for the rainy days while it is still sunny.

46. The Ass Carrying an Image

One day, an ass was given the task of carrying an image to a village temple. He was garlanded with lovely flowers and decorated with exquisite ornaments. As the ass moved along the road, people bowed respectfully and some fell on their knees to show their reverence.

The party slowly moved towards the temple with the priests and other holy people following behind the ass. He was very happy to see people bowing their heads before him. He got the illusion that all respect and honor shown was for him.

The ass so was filled with pride and vanity that he stopped suddenly in the middle of the road and started braying loudly. He refused to proceed any further. His driver understood the scenario immediately.

The driver scorned the ass saying, 'Foolish ass, all this respect and reverence is not for you but for the image that you are carrying. So, walk along and don't get stupid ideas.' The disappointed ass realized his mistake and resumed to walk.

Moral: False assumption and misplaced sense of power is foolishness.

47. A Raven and a Swan

Once, there was a black raven who was envious of a white swan living in a lake. He wanted to turn as white as snow and look like the swan. After pondering a lot, he got the idea that if he lived like the swan, he would turn white like him.

The raven left his home in the forest and flew down to the lake. He started swimming and diving all day long like the swan. He washed himself several times a day, which almost drowned him. He even changed his food habits and started eating water weeds and plants that the swan ate.

But all this washing and swimming did nothing to change his color. Even after days of living in the water, he remained black as ever.

Soon, he grew thin and weak because of the change in his food habits. The water weeds and plants didn't go well with his digestive system. And one day, his weak body could take no more and he breathed his last.

Moral: Your envy can be the cause of your downfall.

48. The Lion and the Gnat

A gnat was buzzing over a lion, stinging him several times. The helpless lion tried to shoo him off, but only managed to injure himself while trying to strike the gnat.

At last, he roared at the gnat angrily, 'Go away, you little thing! Why are you bothering me?'

The gnat replied, 'Do you think I am afraid of you just because they call you the king of the jungle? Today I will show you how weak and helpless you are.'

He kept on stinging the lion. The lion was badly wounded by his own claws because of continuous scratching. Finally, he gave up and left for his den.

The gnat was delighted with his victory over the king. He was filled with pride and wanted to announce the news to the world. He started flying towards his friends but got caught in a spider's web. He tried hard but couldn't get out of it. Within moments, he fell prey to a little spider.

Moral: Foolish pride is harmful.

49. The Rooster and the Jewel

A rooster lived on a farm with other animals. One day, his master was out in the market and couldn't feed him.

The rooster was hungry since morning and was looking for food everywhere. There was not a single grain that he could eat. Finally, he scratched and scraped the earth in the hope of finding some worms or seeds. While doing so, he chanced upon a shining jewel. He pecked at the jewel but for him it was of no value.

He was disappointed and said, 'This jewel might be precious for the owner who lost it. He must be looking for it everywhere in the world. But for me it is completely useless. I can't eat this. I would rather choose a grain of barley instead of this jewel. What a waste!'

He tossed the jewel aside and continued his search for food elsewhere.

Moral: Valuables have no value for those who cannot appreciate them.

50. The Monkey and the Camel

Once, the animals of the jungle organized a party to honor their king, the lion. A monkey was invited for a dance performance. He danced with a lot of grace and style. Everyone was mesmerized by his performance and praised him a lot.

A camel, too, was present at the party and he grew jealous of the monkey. He thought that he could do a better job and was sure that all the animals would appreciate his dance too.

He made his way through the crowd and started dancing on his hind legs. Everyone was horrified to see him perform. He looked clumsy and bulky as he kicked around while twisting his long neck. Silly thing, he had no grace at all!

The animals tolerated his performance for some time, all the while saving themselves from being knocked out by his heavy hoofs. Lost in dancing, the camel came very close to the king. He could have hurt him with his hoofs had the animals not saved him. The animals were furious and chased the camel in the desert.

After some time, the animals at the party enjoyed delicious refreshments that consisted of camel's hump and ribs.

Moral: It is foolish to ape our betters.

51. The Ass, the Fox and the Lion

An ass and a fox were good friends. Though their nature and food habits were completely opposite to each other, yet they always stayed together.

One day, they came across a lion in the forest who was eager to kill one of them for lunch. The ass got frightened but the fox pacified him, 'Don't worry. I will go and talk to him.' The ass trusted the fox.

The fox approached the lion and said, 'O, king of the jungle! I have a great idea! I will send the foolish ass in that deep pit and you can have him for lunch. In return, you have to let me go.' The lion agreed to his plan.

The fox lured the innocent ass into the deep pit, saying that it was a good place to hide.

When the lion saw that the ass was caught in the pit and was ready for taking, he attacked the fox first for betraying his friend.

Moral: Traitors get their due always.

52. The Birds, the Beasts and the Bat

Once upon a time, a fierce battle broke out between the beasts on the land and the birds in the sky. Both the parties killed each other mercilessly. The foxes killed the geese and enjoyed their feast. The owls attacked the mice and ate them.

The hares, chickens, and several other birds and beasts lost their lives in this war. The battle continued for a long time.

The bats played safe in this battle. When they saw that the birds were doing better, they took their side. But when the beasts were winning, the bats supported them. Both the birds and the beasts witnessed this deceitful game quietly.

The war finally got over and peace talks started. Both the parties brought the deceit of the bats to table. It was an unpardonable sin and both the groups refused to accept them in their community. Hence, the bats were driven out from the forest. They were punished to live in deserted ruins and towers and were allowed to hunt only during the night.

Moral: Deceitful ones are not accepted anywhere.

53. The Leap at Rhodes

Once upon a time, there was a man who traveled around the world. When he returned to his native place, people would come to him to listen to his stories. He would tell them about his great adventures and deeds that he had done on his travels.

The man enjoyed the attention that he got. His enthralling stories would mesmerize everyone.

One day, the man was telling the people about a giant leap he had taken in a city called Rhodes. He said, 'The giant leap that I had taken was so great that no one can match it anywhere close to the distance.'

Suddenly, a man stood up and said, 'We understand and believe that you must have taken a giant leap at Rhodes. We would like to witness it ourselves. Can you please repeat that giant leap here?' The man was stunned and was left speechless.

Moral: One should not brag about false achievements.

54. The Lion, the Bear and the Fox

Once, a great bear saw a baby goat near the jungle. He was about to grab the kid when a lion appeared out of nowhere and leaped towards it. Both the lion and the great bear got into a fierce fight. None of them was ready to step back.

The fight continued but not for long. Both of them were badly injured and completely exhausted. They left the kid aside and fell on the ground, gasping for breath.

A sly fox had been observing everything from behind the bushes. He darted in and seizing the kid, vanished within seconds. The bear and the lion could do nothing except gape at the quick fox.

'Had we shared the prize like brothers, we both would have enjoyed it,' they sighed.

Moral: Sometimes those who do all the hard work, do not get to partake in the profit.

55. The Sick Stag

Once, a stag fell sick and had nobody to look after him. He had strength enough to collect food for himself and lie down in a quiet clearing of the jungle and rest. He decided to rest there and eat until his strength returned.

The news of the stag's illness spread fast in the jungle. Many animals decided to pay him a visit to enquire about his health. They went to meet him with goodwill. But while they were engaged in talking with the stag, they carelessly munched on the food that he had collected. Though they meant well, they couldn't stop themselves from finishing off the stag's food.

The poor stag had no energy left to gather more food for himself. Within few days, he starved to death.

Moral: Goodwill should be followed by good deeds.

56. The Wolf and the Sheep

Once upon a time, in the deep jungle, lived a clever wolf. One day, he clashed with the great bear and got injured gravely. He was wounded so badly that he couldn't even walk to the brook, to drink water. He lay exhausted in his lair.

Just then, a sheep passed by his lair and the wolf called out to him for help.

He asked meekly, 'Can you please fetch some water for me from the brook? I am very weak and I need water so that I can gain strength and get some solid food for myself.'

The sheep was no fool. He replied, 'Do you consider me a simpleton? If I get you water, then you won't make any delay in killing me. I will become your solid food.'

The sheep denied the request and walked away. The wolf looked on helplessly.

Moral: Bad intentions are mostly seen through.

57. The Hares and the Frogs

Hares are very meek by nature and they get afraid very easily. Even a slight noise or movement makes them run for cover.

Once, the hares were fed up of their misery and decided to end their lives once and for all. All of them gathered for a meeting to discuss the best way to die. Each one put forward their thoughts while the others listened with complete attention. Suddenly, they heard some noise and within minutes they scampered towards their home.

On the way, they hopped past a pond where a family of frogs was resting on the bank. When the frogs heard this sudden commotion, they jumped into the pond for safety.

One of the hares noticed this and cried, 'Look friends, there are creatures in this world who are afraid of us! We are not the only ones who get scared so easily. We should not feel so bad, after all.'

The hares dropped the idea of ending their lives.

Moral: If we look closely, we will find someone in similar state like ours.

58. The Wolf and the Lion

A wolf caught a lamb from a farm and was merrily carrying it to his lair for lunch. But on the way, he met a lion and stopped in his path. The lion did not wait and snatched the lamb from him.

The wolf was angry but he did not show. He ran to a safe distance to save himself from the lion's wrath. Then, gathering courage, he called out to the lion, 'You have no right to take the lamb away. I stole it and it is mine.'

The lion looked at the wolf scornfully. But the wolf was already quite far away from him and the lion was in no mood to fight. He roared loudly and said, 'It's yours? Did you pay for it to the shepherd or did he gift it to you? Did you buy it from the market? Tell me, how did this become yours?' The wolf had no answer to this.

Moral: One thief is no better than another.

59. The Peacock

Did you know that peacocks used to fly high? But they got bored with it. They wanted to look different and better than other birds.

So one day, a peacock went to God Juno, who loved him more than any other creature, and asked for beautiful feathers. Juno granted his wish and the peacock got a train of colorful feathers. He strutted with pride, as he stood out among all the other birds.

The birds of the jungle admired and envied him for his new precious gift. Even the pheasants could not surpass the peacock's beauty. The bright hues of red, gold, blue, azure and green of the feathers mesmerized everyone.

The peacock was happy, but one day, he saw an eagle soaring high in the sky. The peacock wanted to fly too, as he used to do earlier. But now, with the heavy train of feathers, it was impossible. The weight held him down. He missed the first rays of the morning sky and the floating clouds at sunset that he used to fly up to and enjoy. He could only walk on the ground now. This made the peacock sad.

Moral: Appreciate what you have and be careful what you wish for.

60. The Mice and the Weasels

The mice and the weasels always clashed with each other. The weasels would win every battle and kill the mice in large numbers.

One day, the mice gathered to discuss the problem. They realized that they were being defeated because of the lack of any leader. So, it was decided that the mice army would have leaders to lead them in their battles against the weasels. They appointed many generals and commanders who were learned and experienced.

The newly-appointed leaders wanted to distinguish themselves from the soldiers. Hence, they wore lofty headgears with long feathers and straws.

The mice army started preparing for the war. They trained hard and then sent a challenge to the weasels.

The weasels accepted the challenge and attacked the mice army in huge numbers. Within minutes, the mice army gave up and fled. While running into their holes to save themselves, the junior soldiers slipped in easily. But the generals and commanders got stuck because of their elaborate headgears. The weasels caught them all and had a grand feast.

Moral: With great honor come grave dangers.

61. The Wolf and the Lean Dog

A wolf was prowling around a farm one day. He saw a lean and thin dog lying on the grass. On usual days, the wolf wouldn't care for such a skinny thing but that day he was starving since morning. He decided to kill the dog.

The dog understood the whole situation. He made a proposal to the hungry wolf, 'Dear Lord, I know you are hungry but I have nothing on my body except some bones. My master will soon organize a lavish wedding feast for his only daughter. I will get to eat a lot of leftovers and will fatten myself. So, till then, can you please wait?' The greedy wolf visualized a fat and fleshy dog and let him go.

After a few days, the wolf came to reclaim his prize. He saw the dog inside his master's yard and called out to him. The dog replied, 'Sir, I will come out as soon as our porter opens the door.'

The porter happened to be a ferocious dog who had earlier tried to kill the wolf. The wolf did not wait and quietly decamped.

Moral: Do not be foolish to trust everyone's words.

62. The Vain Jackdaw and His Borrowed Feathers

One day, a jackdaw was flying over the king's palace garden. He happened to look down and saw a party of peacocks enjoying themselves. The jackdaw was filled with envy to see the comfort that the palace offered to all the peacocks. He thought their beautiful plumage allowed them to enjoy the royal treatment.

The jackdaw acted cleverly, picked up some feathers strewn in the garden and stuck them among his own. First, he flew to the other jackdaws to show off his plumage. Then he joined the peacocks in the garden and started walking haughtily among them. The peacocks soon noticed the strange bird and were furious. They attacked the jackdaw and plucked away the feathers, including some of his own.

Injured and hurt, the poor jackdaw went back to his companions. But the other jackdaws were already annoyed with him for trying to be superior to them. They pecked at him and drove him away as a punishment for his silly act.

Moral: Borrowed feathers do not make fine birds.

63. The Fox and the Lion

A young fox was exploring the forest. There were many sights that were completely new to him, but he was more eager to see a lion. Fate favored him and a lion passed before his eyes. The fox immediately ran for shelter for he was quite afraid.

Next day, the fox was roaming around looking for food. This time again, he was lucky to see the same lion drinking water from a stream. The fox stayed back and had a good look at the lion. He was very happy to observe the lion from close quarters.

After a few days, the lion was again spotted resting under a tree. The young fox had become quite bold by now. He was no more afraid of the lion. This time he decided to have a little conversation with him. He walked up to him and said, 'Hello oldie, hope you are doing fine.'

The lion was quite amused and did not bother to reply. The fox, too, turned his tail and went away.

Moral: Familiarity breeds contempt.

64. The Dog and His Master's Dinner

Once, there was a farmer who had kept a dog as a companion. Every day, the dog would carry his master's dinner to the fields. Though the aroma of the food basket tempted the dog, but he never gave in to the temptation.

One day, he was on his usual trip to the fields when several dogs of the neighborhood started following him. They got curious about the basket and soon found out what it contained. They tried their best to steal it but the loyal dog guarded it with his life.

Next day, the dogs made a plan and surrounded him. At first, the dog tried to escape but then he stopped to argue with them.

That was their chance. All of them made the dog feel ridiculous about his loyalty and dutifulness. The dog could take it no more. He dropped the basket and took the roasted steak out and said, 'You all divide the rest of the food.'

Moral: Do not stop to argue with temptation.

65. The Wolf and the Ass

An ass was feeding in a pasture near a jungle. Suddenly, he noticed a wolf lurking behind in the bushes. He immediately cooked up a plan to save himself and started hobbling. It looked as if he was in pain.

The wolf approached him and asked, 'What is wrong with you?'

The ass replied, 'A thorn is stuck in my hind foot. Please take it out for it might choke you when you eat me.'

The wolf asked the ass to show him the thorn. While the wolf was examining the foot, the ass used all his strength to kick his face. The wolf tumbled off quite far away because of the impact. Before he could realize what had happened, the ass had galloped away into the jungle.

The wolf sulked, 'It serves me right. I shouldn't have trusted the ass. My job is to kill animals, not treat them.'

Moral: We should stick to what we are supposed to do.

66. The Monkey and the Cat

A monkey and a cat were very good friends. They lived in a farmer's house as his pets. They were mischievous and greedy.

One evening, the lady of the house had put some chestnuts on the hearth for roasting. The two pals had their eyes on the chestnuts. But they had no idea how to get them.

The monkey said to the cat, 'I would have taken the roasted chestnuts out from the hearth but you are more skilled than me.'

The cat was quite pleased with the compliment. She started drawing hot chestnuts from the hearth a few at a time. It was burning her paws, but she kept doing it with pride. The monkey was quick and started eating those chestnuts.

Suddenly, the master arrived and both the friends took to their heels. The cat realized that she didn't get any chestnuts to eat though she burnt her paws in the process. From that day onwards, their friendship ended forever. She had nothing to do with monkeys anymore. She contented herself with mice and rats.

Moral: The flatterer always takes advantage of the fool.

67. The Dogs and the Fox

Some wild dogs were sniffing around in the jungle. They were very hungry and agitated. Since morning, they had been out looking for prey but had not been able to find anything.

One of them noticed the skin of a lion lying ahead. First, they thought that it was a living lion and tried to hide behind bushes. But soon they realized that it was dead. They walked boldly towards the carcass and in their frustration, started tearing at the skin fiercely.

A wise fox was watching everything from a distance. He said, 'You people are showing your power on a dead lion's skin. If he had been alive, he would have shown his strength to you. His claws and teeth would have dug deeper into your skin than yours.'

The dogs felt ashamed of their actions. They shrugged their shoulders and resumed their search for prey.

Moral: It is very easy and detestable to show your power on a weaker one.

68. The Bear and the Bees

A bear was looking for berries in a forest near a stream. He noticed a hollow log that nestled a beehive filled with honey. He was starving and so decided to have the delicious honey.

The bear peeped inside the hollow log to check if the bees were there. While he was doing so, a swarm of bees returned loaded with fruit nectar to dump in the beehive. They guessed the bear's intentions and attacked him, stinging him black and blue.

The bear got furious and decided to teach the bees a lesson. He jumped on the log and tried to destroy the beehive inside it altogether. This time, the whole swarm of the bees that was inside the log, came flying out and stung the bear all over. The bear ran for his life and managed to save himself by diving in the stream.

Moral: Never give in to anger when your opponent is stronger than you.

69. The Dogs and the Hides

A tanner had put some hides at the bottom of a stream to soak. Some hungry dogs noticed those fine hides and wanted to eat them. Hides make very good meal for dogs. They tried their best to reach them but nothing worked. The stream was deep enough to drown them if they had tried to get down into it.

The dogs held an immediate meeting to think of an idea to obtain those delicious hides. After a long discussion, they concluded that they must drink up the entire water of the stream to reach to the hides. So, they started gulping up the water.

Soon, one after the other, the dogs burst with excess water in their stomachs. Not a single dog was left alive. Still, the level of water in the stream remained as before.

Moral: We should not attempt to do the impossible.

70. The Rabbit, the Weasel and the Cat

Once, a rabbit was invited to a dinner party. He left in a hurry and forgot to lock the front door of his house. A weasel saw the empty house and occupied it.

When the rabbit returned, he saw the weasel comfortably settled in his house. He got annoyed and said, 'Leave my house right now!'

But the weasel said, 'This is my house now. You should leave it at once.'

An old clever cat was observing everything from under a tree. She called out to both the warring parties and offered to settle the dispute.

Both of them agreed and started to speak simultaneously. The cat said, 'Please come near me and speak into my almost deaf ears. I am an old hag now.'

The two of them acted foolish and went close to the cat. In an instant, the cat pounced on them with her sharp claws and teeth, and killed them in one stroke.

Moral: Never trust your enemy to impart justice.

71. The Dog in the Manger

Once, a dog walked inside a farm and was happy to find it empty. The farmer had driven the cattle to the fields for work. The dog went inside the shed and climbed into a manger filled with hay. Finding it very comfortable, he soon dozed off.

He was woken up by the mooing of the cattle that had returned after the day's work. They were very hungry. The dog got up and snarled at the cattle. He didn't allow anyone to come near the manger.

The animals were quite amazed with this strange behavior of the dog. The manger didn't have any meat or bones that could attract him.

The cattle was filled with disgust at the selfish behavior of the dog. One of them said, 'Why are you stopping us? Will you eat the hay in the manger? How selfish of you!'

The dog kept barking at them and soon the farmer heard the noise and came to check. He immediately picked up a stick and drove the dog out of the manger. Later, the dog got a good beating for his selfishness.

Moral: Don't be selfish and deprive others of what you can't even use.

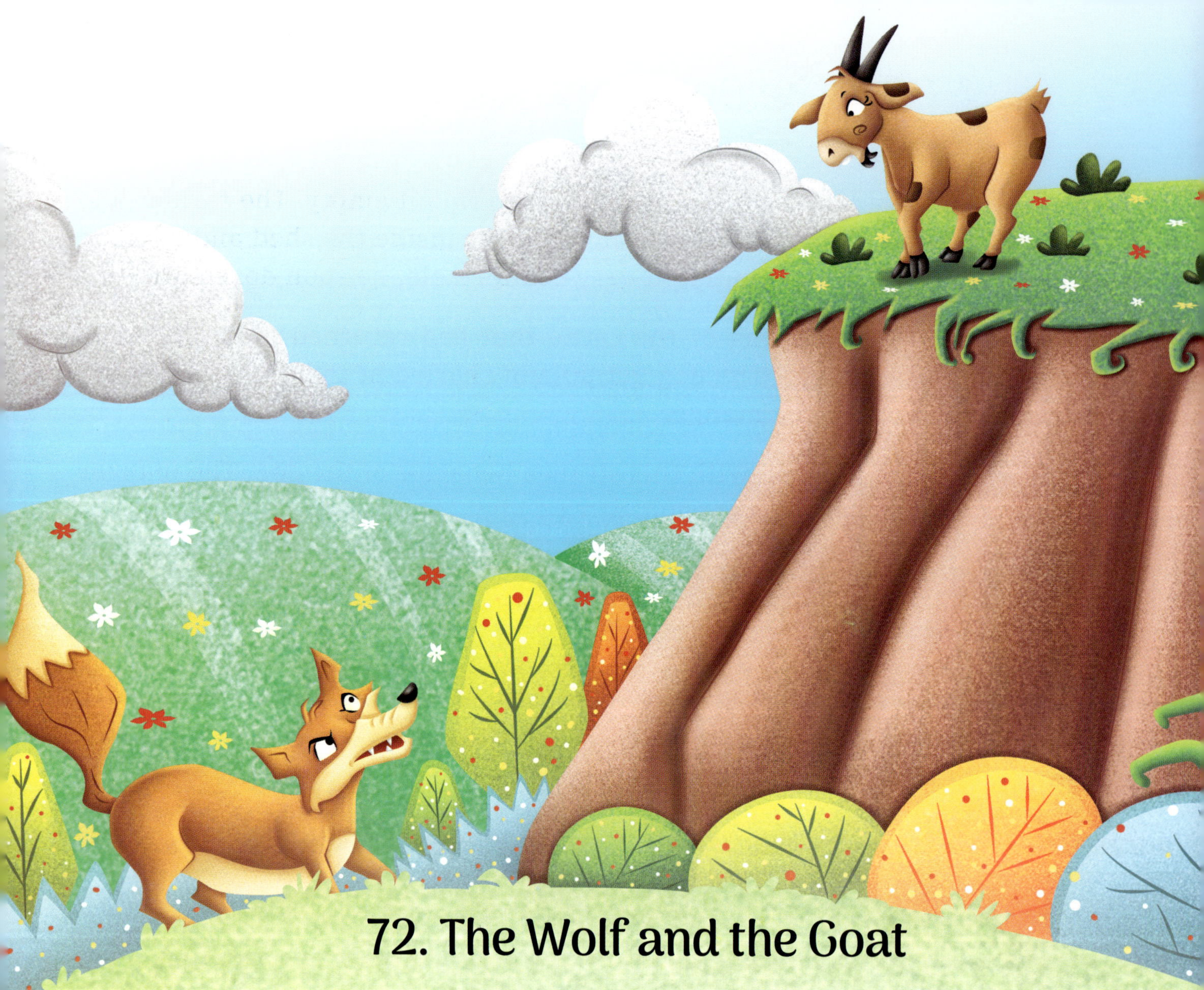

72. The Wolf and the Goat

Once, a hungry wolf was roaming around in search of food. He noticed a fat and healthy goat grazing at the top of a steep cliff. He couldn't have reached her anyhow. So he decided to trap her in his wicked scheme and make her come down to the ground.

He called out to her with a lot of affection and concern in his tone, 'My dear, please come down or you may fall off the cliff. The grass here is greener and abundant. You can eat to your heart's content.'

The goat was no fool and saw through the sweetness of the wolf's tone. She replied with a smile, 'Thank you so much for your concern. But I know that you are not worried about my appetite but yours. You can trap someone else with your falsehood. I know your wicked plan and it won't work on me.'

Poor wolf! He could do nothing and had to leave reluctantly.

Moral: Never trust the sweet words of your enemy.

73. The Ass and the Grasshoppers

An ass was roaming around in the grassy meadows when he heard the merry chirping of the grasshoppers. He was mesmerized by the sweet songs they were singing. His heart was filled with pleasure and he had a sudden urge to sing like them.

He approached the grasshoppers and asked, 'How do you sing so beautifully? What is it that you eat or drink that you have such a heavenly voice? Please tell me. I also want to sing like you.'

The grasshoppers were quite amused to hear this. They decided to play a prank on the ass. One of them replied, 'Of course, we will help you dear friend. If you want to have a voice like us then you should drink the divine dew. You will surely start singing like us in a few days.'

The foolish ass trusted the grasshoppers and stopped eating and drinking everything, except the dew. Soon, he became very frail and died due to starvation.

Moral: Laws of nature can't change, so find your own strength instead of aping others.

74. The Mule

A farmer had kept a mule to carry loads to the market. Most of the days, the mule would eat good food and take long rests. His kind master allowed him the luxury to revive his strength and vigor.

One day, the mule had no work at all. He felt on the top of the world after a long and deep slumber. He felt energetic and jumped all around.

As was his habit, he couldn't keep to himself and told everyone, 'I don't think my predecessors were mere asses. My father must have been a high-spirited horse and I feel the same energy.'

Next day, his master needed his services. The mule was put into harness again and made to carry a heavy load all the way from the field to the market.

That evening, when he returned from work, he was exhausted and low-spirited. The downhearted mule murmured, 'I was mistaken badly, my father was no horse. He was an ass like me, no better.'

He crashed to the ground and slept like a log.

Moral: Don't boast before knowing for sure.

75. The Wolf and the Shepherd

Once upon a time, there was a shepherd who would drive his flock of sheep to the grassy fields near the woods to feed. A wolf was always on the prowl around them but he never harmed any sheep.

In the beginning, the shepherd would get quite anxious and remained on his toes. Gradually, he put his guards down when he noticed that the wolf did not try to come close to the sheep. The shepherd almost started trusting the wolf as if he was his own guard dog. The wolf would also help the shepherd in minding thc flock of sheep.

One day, the shepherd had to go on an important errand. He left the flock of sheep in the pastures, under the care of the wolf. But when he returned, he was devastated to see many sheep dead and several lambs missing. He realized that he had been a fool to trust the wicked wolf.

The shepherd had to return to the farm empty-handed and with a heavy heart.

Moral: Once a wolf, always a wolf.

76. The Farmer and His Sons

A rich farmer was on his deathbed. He wanted his sons to learn an important lesson and called them for an urgent meeting.

He said to them, 'My dear children, I don't have many days to live. Please pay attention to what I say. Never sell the fields to anyone as they are our family property since generations. There is precious treasure hidden somewhere in the fields but I don't know the exact spot. I want you to dig up the fields and look for it.'

The farmer died soon after and the sons began the search for the hidden treasure. They turned up the ground and dug up every nook and corner of the fields but found nothing. Disappointed, they decided to sow seeds in the dug-up fields. They looked after the crops for the whole season and it gave a good yield.

When they harvested the crop and sold it in the market, they earned very good profit. It was greater than any other farmer in the village. The sons realized that the treasure their father was talking about was the wealth of an abundant crop which they earned with their hard work.

Moral: Hard work is in itself a treasure.

77. The Peacock and the Crane

A peacock was proud of his beautiful plumage. He would strut around the barn with his rainbow-colored feathers wide spread. A crane would watch him quietly but never showed any envy or admiration towards him. The peacock felt annoyed at the indifference.

One day, he said to the crane, 'Have a look at my colorful feathers. Look, how beautiful they are! Don't you feel sad that you are cursed with dusty grey wings? No one appreciates you nor likes you.'

The wise crane heard the peacock with a smile. Suddenly, she started flying, higher and higher up in the sky. All the birds including the peacock were filled with envy. As the peacock couldn't fly at all, he was stuck in the barnyard.

'Please follow me if you can,' said the crane from above. 'I feel blessed to have the gift of flight. I am proud of my strong wings and the freedom to fly high.'

Moral: Everyone is unique and gifted.

78. The Farmer and the Cranes

Once, a farmer was sowing his fields with the finest of seeds. A group of clever cranes were watching him closely. They were waiting for him to leave so that they could feast on the seeds.

Finally, the farmer finished his job and left. But he knew the ways of the birds, as he have had bad experience with them in the past too.

As soon as the farmer left, the cranes started digging up the seeds and began eating them. Soon, the farmer came back with a sling in his hand and started swinging it in the air. But he didn't use any stones as he did not want to hurt the birds.

At first, the cranes flew away with fear. But soon they realized that there was no whizzing sound of stone in the air and also not a single bird was getting hurt due to the farmer's action.

Seeing this, many cranes returned to the field and again started digging up the seeds. This time, the farmer got annoyed and used stones to drive them away. Many cranes got severely injured and couldn't fly. The rest fled somehow and decided never to return again.

Moral: Bluff doesn't work with goons.

79. The Goose and the Golden Egg

A farmer once bought a goose and kept it in his farm along with the other animals. Next morning, when he went to check on the goose, he saw that it had laid a golden egg. The farmer went wild with excitement and yelled at his wife, 'It's a golden egg! Come and have a look, dear!'

The farmer's wife came running and was equally amazed to see the egg. The farmer took it to the market and sold it for a lot of money. Every day, the goose would lay a golden egg and the farmer would sell it in the market. Soon, the farmer and his wife became very rich.

But riches brought greed in the wife's mind. One day, she said to the farmer, 'Why do we need to wait every day for a golden egg? Let us cut open the goose and take out all the eggs at once.'

The farmer was convinced with the idea and cut the goose into two with a big knife. Imagine his plight when he found nothing but blood and bones inside! The farmer and his wife cursed themselves for the rest of their lives for their impatience and greed.

Moral: Greed and impatience never pay.

80. The Fighting Bulls and the Frogs

Once, two bulls were fighting in the field. At one corner of the field was a marshy land where many frogs lived with their families. The oldest frog among them was observing the fight and was quite worried.

A young frog noticed the anxious old frog and asked, 'Why are you so worried, uncle? The bulls are fighting far off in the field. They can't cause us any harm.' The old but wise frog replied, 'I am worried for some reason. The bull that loses the fight will be driven away from the fields to the marshy land here. We will all come under his heavy hoofs and get trampled to death. Nobody will be able to save us.'

Soon, the fight got over. Unfortunately, the old frog was right. Not a single frog survived the onslaught of the beaten bull.

Moral: In the battle of the giants, the weak and the innocent always suffer.

81. The Mouse and the Weasel

A hungry mouse was looking for food everywhere. Soon he found a basket of corn in a store room. He squeezed himself through the narrow openings between the strips of the basket.

Once inside, he started gobbling up the corn impatiently. Soon, he was thrice his original size and could hardly move. At last, when he was satisfied, he crawled towards the opening to get out. But all he could do was sneak his head out.

The mouse started panicking. He made all efforts to get out, but in vain. He was finding it too uncomfortable to stay inside the basket.

Just then, a weasel passed by and saw the tiny head of the mouse stuck out of the basket. He guessed the situation and said, 'Greedy fellow, you have been stuffing your tiny stomach so much that you are stuck inside now. You can come out of it only when your stomach goes back to the size it was when you went in. Serves you right! Good night.'

And the weasel left without helping the greedy mouse.

Moral: Greediness always brings problems.

82. The Farmer and the Snake

One cold winter morning, a farmer was going to his fields. Suddenly, he noticed a poisonous snake lying on the ground. The snake was stiff and inactive because of the severe cold.

The farmer knew how deadly snakes can be but then he was a kind man. He couldn't leave the frozen snake to die.

The farmer did the unthinkable. He picked up the snake and put it inside his blazer, next to his bosom. Soon, the snake regained his strength inside the farmer's warm blazer and became active again. The next moment, the snake bit the kind farmer and left.

The dying farmer gasped out these words before he breathed his last. 'Those whose nature is to hurt will always hurt.'

Moral: Never trust the ones whose nature is to hurt.

83. The Goatherd and the Wild Goats

A goatherd was caught in a storm along with his herd of goats. He saw a cave and drove his goats into it for shelter. A few wild goats also took shelter inside the cave to save themselves from the bad weather.

The shepherd was elated to see the wild goats and wanted to make them a part of his herd. He fed them well and gave his own goats just enough to survive. When the weather got cleared, the goats came out to feed themselves.

To the great dismay of the shepherd, the wild goats scampered towards the hilly woods. The shepherd felt cheated. He called them back but the wild goats did not stop.

One of them shouted back at the shepherd, 'We saw how you treated your own herd. You only care for the new ones and want to please them to serve your own selfish interest.'

Moral: It is unwise to treat old friends badly for the sake of new ones.

84. The Cat and the Birds

A cat was growing very thin because of the lack of food. He tried hard but was unable to feed himself properly. One day, he overheard that some birds in the neighborhood were ailing. The hungry cat made a plan to feed himself.

He dressed up in a doctor's white apron, with spectacles on his eyes and carried a leather bag. He went and knocked at the door of the ailing bird family. 'Who's there?' asked the birds.

'A doctor,' replied the cat. 'I heard that someone is ill in the family so I have come to offer assistance. Please open the door and let me examine the ill.'

One of the birds peeped through a hole and saw the cat all dressed up as a doctor. She smiled and shouted from the window, 'We are quite well, doctor. Please don't worry. If you really want us to be healthy, please stay away. Goodbye.'

Moral: We have to be wise and differentiate between a friend and a foe.

85. The Astrologer

Once, there was a man who claimed to be an astrologer. Every night he would gaze at the sky, reading the stars. He boasted of being able to see the future of people in the stars.

One night, he was walking on the country road, his eyes were as usual fixed on the stars. He didn't watch his step and soon found himself in a mud hole.

'Help! Help me!' he started shouting at the top of his voice. Some villagers heard his cries and came running. They used a rope to drag him out of the muddy hole.

Once the astrologer was safe, the villagers started accusing him for his absentmindedness. One of them said, 'You claim to read everybody else's future but you couldn't see your own future and landed in the hole. What is the use of this knowledge if you can't even save yourself from trouble?'

The astrologer was speechless.

Moral: Pay attention to the present, the future will take care of itself.

86. Mercury and the Woodman

A poor woodman was cutting a tree near a river. It was late in the afternoon and he was exhausted. Suddenly, his ax slipped and fell into the river. He started wailing at his loss.

God Mercury heard his cries and appeared to help him. He dived into the river and brought out a golden ax. The woodman refused to take the ax saying it was not his.

Mercury dived again and this time he brought a silver ax. The woodman cried, 'No, my lord, my ax is made of iron with a wooden handle.' Mercury dived for the third time and this time he brought the iron ax. The woodman shed tears of happiness and gratefulness. Mercury was impressed with his honesty and gifted him all the three axes.

This news spread fast in the village and many greedy woodmen went near the river, next day. They hid their axes in the bushes and to cry loudly. Mercury appeared again and got a golden ax from the river for each of them. Each one claimed that it was the one that he had lost.

Mercury was furious at their lies and punished them. Not only did he refuse to give them the golden axes, but also took away their own axes that they had hidden.

Moral: Honesty is the best policy.

87. Three Bullocks and a Lion

Once upon a time, there were three bullocks who were very close friends. They were inseparable and did everything together. They used to graze in an open field where a lion would watch them every day. But he never dared to attack them because he was no match to the three of them together.

Despite knowing that he could never attack them, the lion could not resist the temptation to come to the field every day. He remained hopeful that one day he would grab one of them, if not all.

The lion's patience paid off and that lucky day arrived. The bullocks fought with one another pretty badly and stopped talking to each other. When the hungry lion arrived, he saw the three bullocks at three separate corners of the field. The lion didn't wait for one moment and attacked one of them and killed him immediately.

All the three bullocks were slaughtered one by one, that day.

Moral: In unity lies the strength.

88. The Fox and the Crab

A crab once got bored with the seashore where he had been living all his life. He was fed up with the salty water and the sand mites. He didn't like the sand either, which was his home.

The crab was adventurous and wanted to explore other areas on the land. He wondered about a life away from the shore. He had no idea that life could be difficult or dangerous away from his homeland.

One fine day, he left his home and started his journey towards a meadow not far from the shore. He kept on walking all day. By evening, he reached the meadow and loved the fresh green grass.

Meanwhile, a fox had been noticing him. He was happy with the thought that he is going to have a delicious seafood day. He picked up the crab and gobbled him up in a second.

Moral: Some explorations may not go as you hoped.

89. The Serpent and the Eagle

A snake and an eagle got into a combat. The snake wrapped his body around the eagle and started choking him. The eagle soared in the sky trying to shake off the snake but couldn't free himself. Finally, he flew down to earth as he could no longer breathe.

A man saw this unequal combat and decided to help the noble eagle. He loosened the grip of the snake from the eagle's neck. The snake got furious but couldn't bite the cautious man. When he couldn't reach the man, the snake bit the drinking leather horn tied to the man's belt and filled it with poison.

The man started his return journey towards home. He came across a spring and took out his drinking horn to fill it up. When he wanted to take a sip from the venom-laden horn, the eagle swooped down from nowhere and seized it from the man's hands. He flew away with the horn and dropped it far away, thus saving the man's life.

Moral: Be kind and the world will be kind to you.

90. The Old Lion and the Fox

An old lion had become too frail to catch preys as he used to do in his prime. He feared that he might starve to death. So, he made a plan to pretend to be sick. He made sure that everybody in the jungle was aware of his sickness. Soon, the animals started coming to enquire after his health. The lion invited them inside the den and killed them.

One day, a fox went to visit the lion but he didn't go inside. He stood outside at a safe distance and asked about the well-being of the lion. The lion replied that he was very weak and couldn't come out to meet the fox. He invited the fox to step inside the den so that he could see him better.

The sly fox replied, 'I would love to come inside the den, but before that I have a query. I can see footprints leading into the den but none coming out. How are the visitors getting out of the den?' The lion was speechless.

Moral: Learn from the mistakes of others.

91. The Ass and the Lap Dog

An ass and a lap dog lived at a farmer's house. The farmer loved the dog and gave him delicious treats. The dog, too, loved his master dearly. Every evening, he would wait for him at the door and would frisk around happily upon his return. He would leap upon him playfully to lick his face and hands.

The ass was envious of the way the farmer treated the dog. He never paid any attention to the ass, though he worked the whole day. So, the ass concluded that if he had to seek his master's affection, he should act like the dog.

One day, the ass trotted inside the house and found his master dining. He started frisking around like the dog, upsetting the table as he did so. Then, he rested his forefeet on the master's knees and started licking his face. The master was bewildered. Before he could react, the chair gave in and both of them tumbled over the mess already created.

The farmer was alarmed and called his servants to drag the foolish ass away. The ass was returned to the stable, but only after a good thrashing.

Moral: Imitating someone blindly only brings misfortune.

92. The Goatherd and the Goat

A goat was tempted by a patch of clover and strayed away from the herd to enjoy it. The goatherd tried his best to stop the goat but she paid no attention to his frantic calls.

The goatherd was scared as his master was a strict man. If the master found out that a goat was missing, the goatherd would be punished severely. In an instant, the goatherd picked up a big stone and threw it at the goat.

The stone was thrown with so much power that it hit the goat's horn and broke it into two pieces. The goatherd felt miserable now and started shivering with fear. He said, 'Please, do not tell the master that I broke your horn.'

The goat was in extreme pain. She cried, 'I don't have to say anything to the master. My broken horn will speak for itself.'

Moral: Bad deeds do not stay hidden for long.

93. The Wolf and the Shepherd

A wolf was lurking around a shepherd's house. He could smell the delicious aroma of good food being cooked in the kitchen. He couldn't resist himself and peeped though the window.

The shepherd was sitting in the kitchen at the dining table along with his family. His wife had prepared roasted lamb steaks. The whole family was enjoying the meal together.

The wolf was filled with envy and resentment. Licking his mouth, he muttered, 'How ironical! When I try to catch a lamb for dinner, this man runs after me to stop me with all his might and tricks. And now, he himself has killed a lamb and roasted it for dinner. Hypocrites!'

The wolf returned to the jungle quite sullen.

Moral: We often condemn others for the same thing we do without any remorse.

94. The Mischievous Dog

Once upon a time, there was a mischievous dog who lived in a city. His master was fed up of his bad behavior and mischief. One day, he decided to teach him a lesson. He tied a heavy clog around his neck. The dog had to drag that clog wherever he went and it made a funny noise.

The foolish dog was under the impression that he had been honored. He boasted about that clog to everyone and felt quite superior about it. He had no idea that the opposite was happening.

An old acquaintance came to meet the dog one day. He observed everything and decided to show the light of reason to the dog. He told him, 'Stop strutting around with this clog. It is a sign of disgrace and a proof that you have been an ill-mannered dog. Do you want everyone to know how disgraceful you are?'

The dog hung his head in shame.

Moral: Being notorious doesn't mean that you are famous.

95. The Miser

A miser had hidden a bag of gold coins in his garden. Every day, he went to that secret place, dug up the treasure, counted the gold coins and then put it back.

Once, a thief noticed him and followed him to the garden. He discovered the secret place where the miser had hidden the gold coins. When the time was right, he stole the treasure.

Next day, when the miser discovered the robbery, he was miserable. 'My treasure, someone stole it! It's gone!' he cried.

A passerby heard his cries and asked, 'Did you keep your treasure in that hole? Isn't that foolish of you? You could have kept it safely in your home and spend it whenever you needed it.'

'Why on earth would I spend my treasure?' the miser retorted with anger. 'I would have never touched that gold in my life to buy anything.'

The stranger picked up a stone and threw it inside the hole. 'Cover up that stone, sir. The treasure you lost has the same worth as that stone.'

Moral: Wealth unused might as well not exist.

96. The Cat and the Fox

Once, a cat and a fox were traveling together. While walking, they started talking to pass the time. Soon, their small talk got heated and a serious argument began.

The fox got quite annoyed and said, 'So, you think you are very clever, don't you? You claim that you know more than me. But I know many tricks and far better than you.'

'Yes, I might not be as clever as you. But I know one trick and that's worth a thousand of yours,' the cat retorted sharply.

Just then, they heard a hunter approaching with his pack of hounds. The cat immediately climbed up a tree and hid himself among the leaves. 'This is my trick, now show me yours,' he challenged the fox.

The fox had so many ideas that he got confused which one to use. All his ideas fell flat with the hounds at his heels. Soon, the hounds pounced on him and killed him.

Moral: A single plan that works best is better than hundred unsure ones.

97. The Old Lion

An old lion was on his deathbed. He had grown weak and frail with age. His teeth had fallen off and his claws were worn out. All his past glory had gone into the dust. No one in the jungle feared him anymore. All in all, the king of the jungle had lost his command over the animals that he had enjoyed earlier.

Many animals came to see him breathing his last. The poor lion fell on the ground gasping for breath.

Suddenly, a boar charged towards the dying lion and attacked him with his tusks. The bull also pounced upon him and kicked him with his hoofs. The despicable ass didn't stay behind. He also brayed abuses and kicked the already dying lion.

All the animals remembered the injuries they had borne at the hands of the same old lion. They thought that it was time to take their revenge.

The poor old lion died a miserable death.

Moral: Your actions are always remembered.

98. The Sheep and the Pig

One day, a farmer was at his farm, working. A little pig arrived there from a nearby jungle. The poor thing had lost his way and was very scared.

The farmer was elated to see the pig. He decided to sell him to the butcher and make some extra money. He grabbed the pig and tucked him under his arm. The little pig squealed at the top of his voice but the farmer paid no heed.

This amused the flock of sheep at the farm. One of them asked the pig, 'Why are you so afraid? The farmer catches us in the same manner everyday but we don't shout at all.'

The pig cried in response, 'The farmer doesn't catch you to kill but to shave your wool. He will take me to the butcher and I will be killed soon.'

The little pig kicked and shrieked but in vain.

Moral: It is easy to be brave when faced with no danger.

99. The Ass in the Lion's Skin

An ass found a lion's skin left in the forest by a hunter. He wore the skin and hid himself in a thicket. He decided to scare the other animals of the jungle and have fun that day.

Whenever an animal came near the thicket, the ass would jump out and frighten the animal away. The animals would run for their lives without looking back once.

The ass started enjoying the prank. This continued for some time. He was so involved into the prank that he forgot his own identity. After scaring a fresh batch of animals, he couldn't control himself anymore. He expressed his joy by braying out loudly and clearly.

The fox who was running away from him, stopped midway. He heard the bray and realized that it was an ass under a lion's skin.

He told the ass, 'You should have kept your mouth shut if you wanted us to be afraid of you. Now, it won't work. Your secret is out.'

Moral: You can deceive people by your looks but your words reflect the reality.

100. The Fox and the Monkey

It was election time and the jungle was all decked up. All the animals had gathered to elect their new king. The monkey was asked to present a dance. He danced quite gracefully and everyone enjoyed and appreciated it. All the animals unanimously voted for the monkey except for the fox. The monkey was elected as the new king.

The fox was quite annoyed with the animals for electing an unworthy ruler. One day, he saw a metal trap with a piece of meat attached as bait. He immediately went to the monkey and told him that a rich treasure was waiting for him.

The greedy monkey king left hurriedly with the fox to collect the treasure. When they reached there, the monkey tried to grasp the meat and his hand got stuck in the trap.

The fox laughed and said, ‘You can’t take care of yourself and you pretend to be our king. You have no brains at all.’

Later, another meeting was called to elect a new ruler.

Moral: A true leader has to prove their worth by their qualities and not gimmicks.

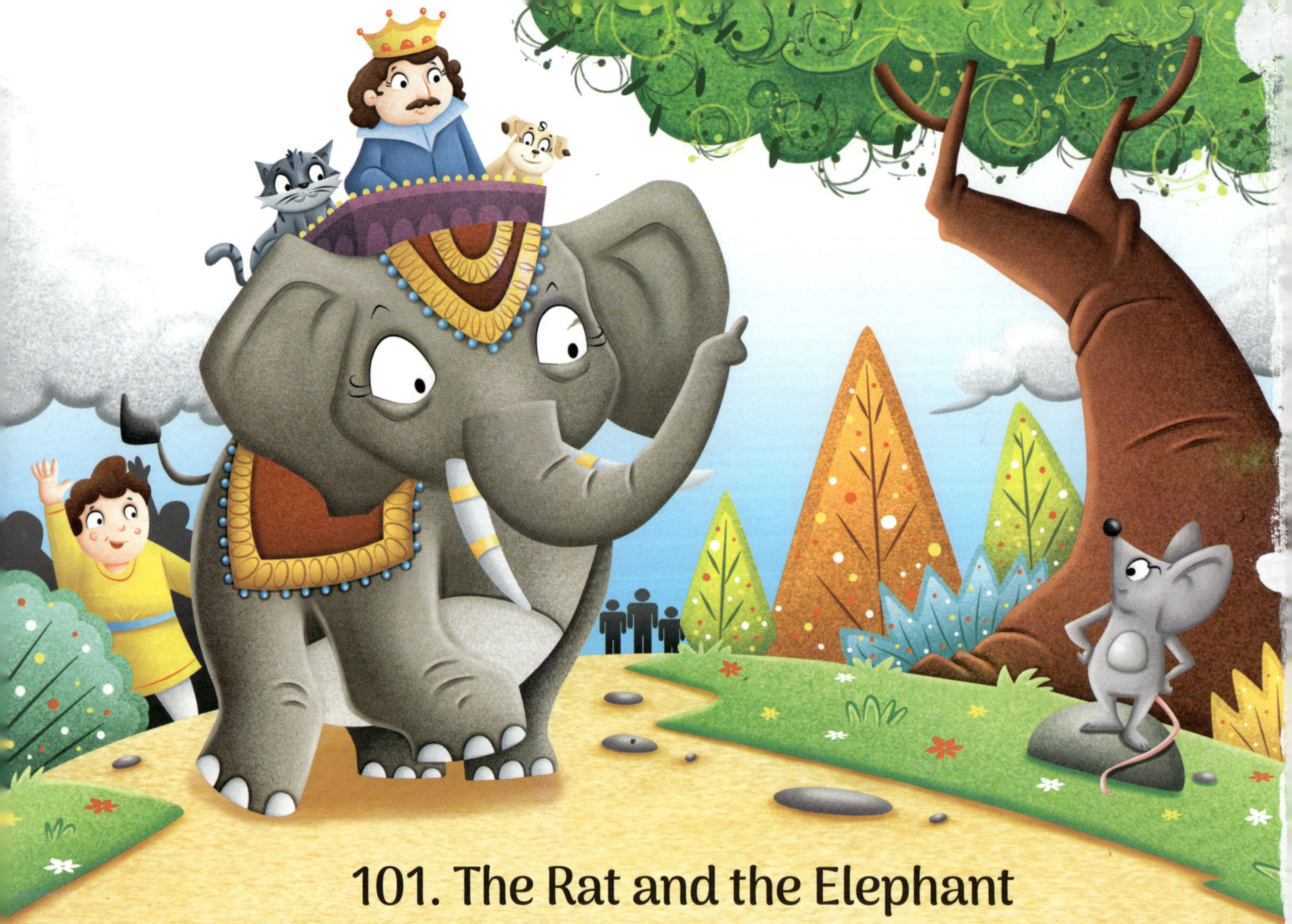

101. The Rat and the Elephant

There was once a haughty rat who thought himself to be the most important one. He walked with an air of superiority. One day, while he was walking on the roadside, he saw a procession of people. It was the king and his followers.

The king was riding an elephant that had been beautifully decorated. The elephant was adorned with lovely flowers and gorgeous trappings. The king's royal dog and cat were also seated with him.

The rat noticed that the people walking in the procession and those looking on from the roadside were admiring the elephant. Nobody noticed the tiny rat.

The rat's pride was hurt and he muttered, 'Foolish people! They are appreciating a clumsy elephant with huge ears and wrinkled skin. I have ears, eyes and legs, too. Only if they could realize my worth and importance, they would all follow me.'

While he was engrossed in thinking about himself, the royal cat pounced upon him and gulped him down instantly.

Moral: Don't get carried away by the resemblance only to lose in reality.